Tiger

Nick Butterworth

HarperCollins *Children's Books*

This is Tiger.

He isn't a real tiger.
He's a kitten.
But sometimes,
when he plays,
he pretends to be
a *real* tiger.

He pretends
that his soft, little,
tigery paws...

...are great, big,
tigery claws!

He pretends
that his funny, little,
tigery miaow...

...is a loud,
scary, tigery
ROAR!

Tiger is
very good
at jumping...

...just like
a real tiger!

And Tiger is
very good at
creeping up on things.
He can be as quiet

as a mouse...

...just like
a real tiger!

Tiger doesn't
play with wool.

Real tigers don't play with wool.

And if Tiger gets a sudden surprise, he is **EXTRAORDINARILY** fast at getting away...

...just like
a real tiger!

And at the end
of a long day of
jumping and snarling
and very fast running
and quiet creeping and
not playing with wool,
Tiger really likes
his bed...

...just like a real tiger!

... So I said to him, I said, "Now look here, Stripey," I said...

First published in hardback in Great Britain by HarperCollins Children's Books in 2006
First published in paperback in 2006
This edition published specially for Bookstart in 2007

1 3 5 7 9 10 8 6 4 2

ISBN-13: 978-0-00-778470-7
ISBN-10: 0-00-778470-8

Text and illustrations copyright © Nick Butterworth 2006

HarperCollins Children's Books is a division of HarperCollins Publishers Ltd.

Visit our website at: www.harpercollinschildrensbooks.co.uk

Printed and bound in Singapore